Advancing Patient Quality and Safety:

A Scalable Framework for Transformation

By

A.H. Nguyen, MD, MBA, CPPS, FABC, FACS

Case ID: 1-15003674757

Paperback ISBN: 978-1-969775-16-1

Table of Contents

Dedication

For Dr. Peter Tu Bui, my dear friend, my trusted colleague, and a consummate human being.

You were the kind of person who made everyone around you better— not by demanding it, but by living it. Your integrity was quiet but unwavering. Your kindness was effortless and constant. And your wisdom—always offered with humility—left a mark on every room you entered.

This book is for you because so much of what I believe about patient care, leadership, and humanity was shaped by watching you live those values every day.

Thank you for being my friend. Thank you for being the kind of person this world so desperately needs. This is for you.

—A.H. Nguyen

Acknowledgments

No work of this scale is ever truly written alone. It is shaped by conversations, challenged by questions, and sustained by the quiet encouragement of those who believe in you—especially when you begin to doubt yourself.

To my colleagues and friends: Tina Williams, Kristina Cartwright, Joan Deal, Helena Walo Bates, and Carol Stefaniak—thank you for your wisdom, your candor, and your unwavering commitment to making healthcare better. You've each taught me something invaluable: how to lead with integrity, how to listen with intention, and how to never lose sight of the people behind the process. Your support throughout this journey has meant more than I can express.

To my wife, Hieu—Thank you for your support and strength. Your patience has been quiet but unwavering. Your guide has been steady, even when the path was uncertain.

And to my daughter, Zoe—you are the reason I care so deeply about the future. Your curiosity, your joy, and your boundless imagination remind me every day why this work matters. I hope this book helps build a world where care is safer, kinder, and more human—for you and for everyone.

Thank you all for walking beside me. This book carries your fingerprints, your voices, and your spirit. I'm proud to share it with you.

Foreword

I didn't write this book because I had all the answers. I wrote it because I've lived the questions.

Over the past three decades, I've stood at the bedside during moments of heartbreak and healing. I've sat in boardrooms where strategy was debated, and in break rooms where courage was quietly practiced. I've seen what happens when systems fail—and what's possible when they rise to meet the moment.

Patient safety, for me, has never been an abstract concept. It's the mother whose voice wasn't heard. It's the nurse who caught a near-miss and stayed late to make sure it didn't happen again. It's the surgical tech who spoke up, even when it was uncomfortable. It's the administrator who chose integrity over expedience. These are the people who taught me what safety really means.

This book is my attempt to honor them—and to equip others with the tools to lead with the same conviction.

The framework I present here is not theoretical. It's built from the ground up, shaped by real-world challenges and refined through trial, error, and iteration. It's designed to be scalable because I've worked in places where resources were scarce and expectations were high. It's designed to be adaptable because no two organizations—or communities—are the same. And it's designed to be human because data alone doesn't save lives—people do.

If you're reading this, you're likely someone who cares deeply about the future of healthcare. You may be a clinician, a leader, a policymaker, or a patient advocate. You may be exhausted, hopeful, skeptical, or all three. Wherever you are, I want you to know: you are not alone.

Transformation is not a solo act. It's a collective movement. And it begins with a single decision—to lead with purpose.

So, I invite you to take this framework and make it your own. Use it to spark conversations, challenge assumptions, and build systems that reflect the dignity of those they serve. Let it be a compass when the path is unclear, and a rallying cry when the work feels heavy.

Because the future of patient safety isn't something we inherit—it's something we build. Together.

—Dr. A.H. Nguyen

Introduction: The Inflection Point

The U.S. healthcare system stands at a pivotal moment—one defined not just by complexity, but by consequence. For decades, the pursuit of patient safety and quality improvement has been marked by incremental progress. These gains were hard-won, driven by rigorous research, evolving regulations, and the tireless efforts of clinicians, administrators, and advocates who believed that better was always possible.

Yet today, the landscape is shifting more rapidly than ever before. The forces reshaping healthcare are not subtle—they are seismic. Rising labor and supply costs, widespread workforce shortages, and increasing fragmentation across care delivery systems have created a perfect storm. These pressures threaten to stall—or even reverse—the progress we've made in improving patient outcomes, reducing harm, and building cultures of safety.

The COVID-19 pandemic was both a catalyst and a crucible. It laid bare the vulnerabilities of our healthcare infrastructure, strained resources to their breaking point, and disrupted workflows that had long been taken for granted. It exposed systemic inequities that had lingered in the shadows and brought them into sharp relief. Rates of hospital-acquired conditions and adverse events surged. Burnout became endemic. And while recent data suggests a modest recovery, the underlying issues remain unresolved.

This is not a moment for incrementalism. It is a moment for transformation.

To navigate this inflection point, healthcare organizations must adopt a new mindset—one that embraces scalability, data-driven decision-making, and operational discipline. We must move beyond isolated interventions and toward integrated systems. We must shift from reactive problem-solving to proactive design. And we must recognize that safety is not a department—it is a philosophy that must permeate every corner of the organization.

This book offers a framework designed to help institutions reach what we call the *Quality And Safety Frontier*—a concept borrowed from Michael Porter's Productivity Frontier work in competitive strategy(Porter, M. E. (1996). What Is Strategy? Harvard Business Review, 74(6), 61–780). In healthcare, this *Frontier* represents the optimal balance between efficiency and excellence: delivering the highest quality care at the lowest possible cost per unit. It is not a theoretical ideal—it is an achievable reality, but only for organizations willing to rethink how they operate, how they lead, and how they learn.

The chapters ahead will guide you through a three-step transformation model:

1. **Identify the Customer**: Understand who you serve, what they need, and where the risks lie.
2. **Implement Essential Components**: Build the operating, data, and management systems that support scalable change.
3. **Operationalize the Framework**: Embed safety and quality into the daily rhythm of care.

This model is supported by real-world examples, actionable tools, and a field-tested methodology drawn from years of experience across diverse healthcare settings. It is designed to be practical, adaptable, and scalable—whether you're leading a rural hospital, a multi-site health system, or a specialized clinical unit.

Whether you're a hospital CEO, a frontline nurse, a quality improvement specialist, or a patient advocate, this book is your roadmap to redefining what's possible in patient care. It is a call to action, a guide to execution, and a blueprint for building a future where safety is not just expected—but guaranteed.

Let's move the *Frontier*—together.

Part I: Foundations of Patient Quality and Safety

Chapter 1: The Evolution of Patient Safety

From Florence Nightingale to the Quality And Safety Frontier

Patient safety is not a trend—it is a moral imperative that has shaped the very foundation of modern medicine. Its roots stretch back centuries, long before the term "quality improvement" entered the healthcare lexicon. At its core, patient safety is about honoring the trust placed in caregivers and ensuring that the act of healing does not inadvertently cause harm.

The Origins: Florence Nightingale and the Birth of Evidence-Based Care

In the mid-19th century, Florence Nightingale revolutionized battlefield medicine during the Crimean War. Armed not with advanced technology but with meticulous observation and an unwavering commitment to hygiene, she documented infection rates, mortality patterns, and environmental conditions. Her insistence on cleanliness, ventilation, and nutrition dramatically reduced death rates—and laid the groundwork for what we now call epidemiology.

Nightingale's legacy was more than clinical—it was cultural. She demonstrated that data could drive decisions, that systems mattered as much as skill, and that compassion and rigor were not mutually exclusive. Her work planted the seed for a movement that would take over a century to fully blossom.

The Awakening: To Err Is Human and the Safety Movement

In 1999, the Institute of Medicine published To Err Is Human, a landmark report that sent shockwaves through the healthcare community. It is estimated that nearly 100,000 deaths occur annually in U.S. hospitals due to preventable medical errors, making medical harm one of the leading causes of death.

The report did more than expose a crisis—it catalyzed a movement. Suddenly, patient safety was no longer a quiet concern whispered among clinicians. It became a national priority. Policymakers, hospital executives, and professional societies began to take notice. The era of safety science had arrived.

The Response: Regulation, Technology, and Transparency

Over the next two decades, a wave of reforms reshaped the healthcare landscape. Organizations like the Centers for Medicare & Medicaid Services (CMS), The Joint Commission, and the Leapfrog Group introduced new standards, incentives, and public reporting mechanisms. Hospitals began tracking adverse events, implementing surgical checklists, and investing in electronic health records.

Simulation labs were built. Root cause analysis became routine. Safety huddles emerged. And yet, despite these efforts, progress remained uneven. Some institutions achieved remarkable reductions in harm, while others struggled to move the needle. The reasons were complex, ranging from resource limitations to cultural resistance to change.

The Shift: Value-Based Care and the Integration Imperative

In the 2010s, the rise of value-based care added a new layer of complexity. Safety was no longer a standalone goal—it became intertwined with reimbursement, patient satisfaction, and population health. Hospitals were now paid not just for what they did, but for how well they did it—and whether patients stayed healthy after discharge.

This shift demanded a more integrated approach. Safety could no longer live in a silo. It had to be embedded in every aspect of care delivery—from scheduling and staffing to discharge planning and community outreach. It required collaboration across departments, alignment between clinical and financial goals, and a renewed focus on outcomes that matter to patients.

The Challenge Today: Scaling Safety Across Systems

Despite the progress, today's healthcare systems face a daunting challenge: how to improve safety at scale, across diverse settings, with limited resources. The pandemic exacerbated existing vulnerabilities, strained workforces, and exposed gaps in coordination. Burnout surged. Trust eroded. And yet, the need for transformation has never been more urgent.

This is where the concept of the Quality And Safety Frontier becomes essential.

It offers a new lens—a way to think about safety not just as a compliance requirement, but as a strategic opportunity. It challenges organizations to deliver the highest possible quality at the lowest possible cost, using the resources they have today. And it invites leaders to reimagine what's possible when safety is treated not as a burden, but as a catalyst for excellence.

Field Notes The evolution of patient safety is not a linear story—it's a tapestry woven from courage, data, failure, and resilience. From Nightingale's battlefield to the boardrooms of modern health systems, the journey has been marked by breakthroughs and setbacks. But the destination remains clear: a healthcare system where safety is not just expected—but guaranteed.

Notes

Chapter 2: The Productivity Frontier in Healthcare

Reaching the Edge of What's Possible—and Redefining It

The Productivity Frontier is a concept borrowed from business strategy, but its implications in healthcare are far more profound. In traditional industries, it marks the outer boundary of efficiency and value—where a company delivers the highest quality at the lowest cost, given its current capabilities. In healthcare, however, the stakes are higher. Here, the *Frontier* represents the maximum level of patient outcomes, safety, and experience that can be achieved per unit of care—without compromising compassion, equity, or dignity.

It is not a theoretical ideal. It is a measurable, achievable threshold. But most healthcare organizations operate well below it.

Despite decades of reform efforts, the system remains riddled with inefficiencies. Redundant workflows, fragmented communication, and misaligned incentives create friction at every level. Excellence exists—but it's unevenly distributed. One unit may deliver world-class care while another struggles with basic coordination. This inconsistency breeds variation—not just in clinical outcomes, but in how patients experience care, how staff feel about their work, and how leaders measure success.

The reasons are complex. Healthcare is not a single system—it's a constellation of cultures, technologies, and human relationships. It's shaped by regulatory pressures, reimbursement models, and legacy infrastructure. But at its core, the gap between current performance and the frontier is not just technical—it's cultural. It reflects how organizations think, how they lead, and how they learn.

To close that gap, organizations must pursue a dual strategy—one that balances discipline with imagination, and optimization with innovation.

1. Optimize Existing Best Practices

Optimization is about discipline. It means identifying what works—and doing it consistently. It's the art of eliminating waste, reducing variation, and aligning teams around shared goals. It's Lean thinking applied to clinical care. It's making sure that every patient benefits from the best-known methods, not just the lucky ones who happen to land in high-performing pockets of the system.

Optimization is not glamorous. It's often slow, meticulous, and uncelebrated. But it's foundational. Without it, innovation becomes decoration—bright ideas layered on top of broken systems. Optimization builds the scaffolding for reliability. It creates the conditions for excellence to be repeatable, not accidental.

Examples include:

- Standardizing handoff protocols to reduce communication errors
- Embedding checklists into high-risk procedures
- Aligning documentation workflows to reduce cognitive load

These are not revolutionary changes—but they are transformative when applied with rigor and consistency.

2. Innovate Beyond Current Boundaries

Optimization alone won't get us to the *Frontier*. We must also leap forward. That means reimagining care delivery through data, technology, and human ingenuity. It means using predictive analytics to anticipate deterioration, virtual platforms to expand access, and artificial intelligence (AI) to support clinical decision-making. It means empowering patients with tools that make them active participants in their care.

Innovation must be inclusive. It cannot be reserved for pilot programs or flagship hospitals. It must be scalable, equitable, and grounded in the realities of frontline care. It must be designed not just for efficiency—but for empathy.

Examples include:

- Deploying remote monitoring for chronic disease management
- Using machine learning to identify patients at risk for readmission
- Creating digital twins to simulate care pathways before implementation

Innovation is not about chasing novelty—it's about solving real problems in new ways.

A Cultural Shift Is Non-Negotiable

This dual approach demands more than operational change—it requires a transformation in mindset. Leaders must stop treating safety as a regulatory checkbox and start seeing it as a strategic asset. Staff must be empowered to speak up, challenge norms, and lead improvement. And organizations must embrace transparency—not just in metrics, but in failures, near-misses, and lessons learned.

Culture is the invisible infrastructure of performance. It determines whether teams feel safe to report errors, whether leaders respond with curiosity or punishment, and whether improvement is seen as a shared responsibility or someone else's job.

A culture of safety is not built overnight. It requires:

- Psychological safety at every level
- Leadership visibility and vulnerability
- Rituals of reflection and learning

Without culture, systems fail. With culture, systems evolve.

The Framework That Follows

This is where the framework presented in this book becomes essential.

It is not a one-size-fits-all solution. It is a flexible, scalable guide designed to meet organizations where they are—and help them move toward where they could be. It's built on real-world experience, not theory. It's informed by frontline voices, not just executive vision. And it begins with a deceptively simple question: *Who are we caring for?*

Because the journey to the *Frontier* is not just about systems—it's about people. It's about the mother in the emergency room, the nurse on the night shift, the technician who catches a mistake, and the administrator who refuses to accept "good enough." It's about building a healthcare system that doesn't just aim for excellence—but expects it.

The Quality And Safety Frontier is not a finish line—it's a mindset. It's a commitment to continuous improvement, radical empathy, and strategic courage. And it's within reach.

<u>Notes</u>

Part II: The Framework for Transformation

Chapter 3: Step 1 – Identify the Customer

Understanding Who We Serve—and Why It Matters

Transformation begins with clarity. In healthcare, that clarity starts with understanding the people we serve—not just as patients, but as individuals embedded in families, communities, and systems. They are shaped by social determinants, influenced by cultural norms, and affected by systemic inequities. Identifying the customer is not a marketing exercise—it's a strategic imperative. It's the first and most essential step in designing care that is safe, equitable, and effective.

Too often, healthcare organizations launch quality initiatives without fully understanding the populations they aim to impact. They rely on assumptions, averages, and outdated data. The result is misaligned interventions, wasted resources, and missed opportunities. To truly transform care, we must begin by asking: *Who are we caring for? What do they need? And what stands in their way?*

Conducting a Community Needs Assessment (CNA)

A Community Needs Assessment is the lens through which we see the broader context of care. It's not just a compliance requirement—it's a compass. It reveals gaps in access, disparities in outcomes, and barriers that prevent patients from receiving timely, effective treatment. A robust CNA is both quantitative and qualitative, both analytical and empathetic.

Key components include:

- **Quantitative Data** This includes prevalence rates of chronic conditions like diabetes, hypertension, and chronic obstructive pulmonary disease (COPD);

behavioral health indicators such as depression and substance use; and utilization patterns across emergency departments, primary care, and specialty services.

- **Qualitative Insights** Data alone doesn't tell the whole story. Interviews with community leaders, patient advocates, public health officials, and faith-based organizations provide context, nuance, and lived experience. These voices help us understand not just what is happening—but *why*.

- **SDOH Mapping** Social determinants of health—housing, food security, transportation, education, and employment—are powerful predictors of outcomes. Mapping these factors geographically helps identify high-risk zones and tailor interventions accordingly.

- **Equity Analysis:** Disaggregated data by race, ethnicity, income, language, and geography uncovers hidden disparities. It allows organizations to move beyond surface-level metrics and address the root causes of inequity.

Field Insight: A CNA is not a one-time report—it's a living document. It should be revisited regularly, updated with new data, and used to guide strategic decisions across departments.

Analyzing Patient Demographic and Clinical Data

Once we understand the community, we turn inward. Internal data reveals who is walking through our doors and what they need. This analysis must be granular, dynamic, and actionable.

Key dimensions include:

- **Demographics:** Age distribution, gender identity, language preference, payer mix, and geographic origin all influence care needs and access barriers.

- **Risk Stratification** Using Hierarchical Condition Categories (HCCs) coding, predictive models, and registries, organizations can identify high-risk cohorts—patients with multiple comorbidities, frequent admissions, or complex social needs.
- **Care Patterns** Trends in readmissions, adverse events, length of stay, and disease progression help pinpoint where systems are failing and where opportunities for improvement exist.
- **Segmentation by Setting:** Different care settings require different strategies. Inpatient, ambulatory, emergency, post-acute, and home health populations each have unique workflows, risks, and resource needs.

Field Insight: Internal data must be dynamic, not static. It should inform real-time decision-making and long-term planning. Dashboards, registries, and predictive tools must be accessible to frontline teams—not just analysts.

Aligning with Strategic Growth and Business Development

Quality and safety don't exist in a vacuum. They must be aligned with organizational strategy. When quality initiatives are disconnected from business development, they risk becoming unsustainable. When aligned, they become engines of growth and impact.

This alignment includes:

- **Collaborating with Strategy Teams** to understand future expansions, joint ventures, and service line priorities. If a hospital is building a new cardiac center, quality teams should be involved from day one.
- **Analyzing Referral Patterns** Track shifts in volume, acuity, and payer mix. Are more patients coming from rural areas? Are referrals increasing for behavioral

health? These trends inform resource allocation and workforce planning.

- **Market Scanning:** Evaluate demographic shifts, employer health plan changes, and migration patterns. Anticipate future needs, not just current ones.

Field Insight: When quality is aligned with growth, it becomes sustainable. It delivers clinical impact and strategic value. It earns the trust of both patients, families, friends, and cross-industry stakeholders.

Field Notes Relevance Is the Foundation

Understanding your patient population is not a preliminary step—it's the foundation. It ensures that every intervention, every investment, and every innovation is rooted in relevance. It transforms care from generic to personalized, from reactive to proactive, and from fragmented to integrated.

This step is not just about data—it's about empathy. It's about seeing patients not as cases, but as people. And it's about designing systems that honor their complexity, respect their dignity, and meet them where they are.

<u>Notes</u>

Chapter 4: Step 2 – Implement Essential Components

Building the Infrastructure for Transformation

Once we've identified the populations we serve and the outcomes we aim to achieve, the next step is to construct the systems that make transformation possible. These systems—Operating, Data, and Management—are not isolated silos. They are deeply interdependent, forming the infrastructure that supports safety, quality, and efficiency across the continuum of care.

Think of them as the scaffolding of a high-performing health system. Without them, even the most visionary strategies will falter. With them, organizations can move from reactive problem-solving to proactive excellence.

<u>a) Operating System: The Architecture of Safety</u>

The Operating System defines how care is delivered. It's the blueprint for clinical workflows, communication, and accountability. But more than that, it's the emotional and psychological framework that determines whether staff feel safe, supported, and empowered.

Key components include:

- Transparent Reporting: A culture of safety begins with visibility. Staff must be able to report safety events, near misses, and concerns without fear of punishment. Reporting systems should be intuitive, accessible, and seamlessly integrated into daily routines—not hidden behind bureaucracy. When reporting is normalized, learning becomes continuous.
- Harm Classification Models: Not all safety events are equal. Classification tools help organizations triage

issues based on severity, frequency, and preventability. This allows leaders to allocate resources wisely, focus on high-impact interventions, and track progress over time. These models also support strategic planning by identifying systemic vulnerabilities.

- Psychological Safety Structures: Safety is not just procedural—it's relational. Staff must feel psychologically safe to speak up, challenge assumptions, and share concerns. This requires visible leadership commitment, structured debriefs after critical events, and feedback loops that demonstrate responsiveness. When trust is built into the system, engagement follows.

Field Insight: The Operating System is not just a set of protocols—it's a reflection of organizational values. When staff trust the system, they participate in it. When they participate, safety improves.

b) Data System: The Engine of Improvement

Data is not just a record of what happened—it's a tool for shaping what happens next. A robust Data System transforms raw information into actionable insights, enabling organizations to anticipate risk, measure performance, and drive continuous improvement.

Core elements include:

- Centralized Repositories: Fragmented data leads to fragmented care. Safety and quality data must be integrated across departments and disciplines, creating a single source of truth. This enables cross-functional analysis and supports enterprise-wide learning.
- Predictive Analytics: The future of safety is anticipatory. Validated algorithms can identify patients at risk for falls, infections, or readmissions—before

harm occurs. These tools must be transparent, explainable, and embedded in clinical workflows to be truly effective.

- Benchmarking Tools: Internal metrics are important, but external comparisons drive excellence. Benchmarking against national standards and peer institutions fosters accountability, highlights gaps, and inspires innovation. It also helps organizations understand what "good" looks like—and how to get there.

Field Insight: Data must be democratized. It should be accessible to frontline teams, not just analysts. When data informs decisions at every level, improvement becomes everyone's job.

<u>c) Management System: The Culture Engine</u>

If the Operating System is the architecture and the Data System is the engine, the Management System is the soul. It's where people, purpose, and performance converge. This system focuses on developing human capital, aligning teams, and translating strategy into daily action.

Essential components include:

- Just Culture Principles: A Just Culture balances accountability with learning. Staff must feel confident that errors will be treated fairly—not punitively. This encourages transparency, supports psychological safety, and reinforces the idea that mistakes are opportunities for growth.
- Training Programs: Transformation requires new skills. Staff must be equipped in scientific problem-solving, team dynamics, and systems thinking. These competencies enable frontline teams to identify root causes, test solutions, and sustain improvements.

- Leadership Structures: Alignment is everything. Tiered huddles, escalation pathways, and shared goals ensure that strategic priorities are connected to frontline realities. Leaders must be visible, responsive, and fluent in both clinical and operational language.

Field Insight: The Management System is where culture lives. It's where values become behaviors, and where strategy becomes execution.

Field Notes Building with Intention

These systems are not optional—they are essential. They must be built with intention, maintained with discipline, and refined with feedback. Organizations that treat them as afterthoughts will struggle. Those who invest in them will thrive.

Together, the Operating, Data, and Management Systems form the backbone of transformation. They enable scale, sustain momentum, and ensure that safety and quality are not just goals—but realities.

Notes

Chapter 5: Step 3 – Operationalizing the Framework

Turning Strategy into Daily Practice

Once the foundational systems—Operating, Data, and Management—are in place, the final and most critical step is integration. Operationalizing the framework means embedding it into the daily rhythm of care. It's not a one-time rollout, a quarterly initiative, or a leadership retreat topic. It's a cultural shift that must be sustained, visible, and reinforced across every layer of the organization.

This step is where transformation becomes tangible. It's where abstract principles meet real-world complexity, and where systems begin to shape behaviors, decisions, and outcomes. Operationalization is not about perfection—it's about persistence. It's about showing up every day with intention, discipline, and a shared commitment to safety.

Daily Safety Leadership Huddles

These huddles are the heartbeat of a high-reliability organization. They are short, structured meetings—often held at the start of each shift—where leaders and frontline staff come together to review safety events, discuss emerging risks, and align on priorities.

The power of the huddle lies in its consistency. It creates a cadence of accountability and a shared language around safety. It reinforces the idea that safety is not a department—it's a daily practice.

Effective huddles are:

- **Inclusive:** Nurses, physicians, environmental services, transport, and administrative staff all have a voice.

- **Focused:** They prioritize real-time issues, not theoretical discussions.
- **Actionable:** They generate follow-ups, assign responsibilities, and close the loop.

Over time, huddles build psychological safety, foster transparency, and strengthen team cohesion. They turn safety from a concept into a conversation.

Field Insight: The best huddles are not perfect—they're persistent. They create space for learning, listening, and leading.

Electronic Event Tracking

Digital tools are essential for capturing, analyzing, and responding to safety events. A robust electronic reporting system allows staff to document incidents in real time, categorize them by severity, and trigger appropriate follow-up.

These systems should be:

- **Intuitive:** Easy to use, with minimal friction.
- **Accessible:** Available across devices and departments.
- **Integrated:** Embedded into clinical workflows, not bolted on.

Beyond documentation, electronic tracking enables trend analysis. Are medication errors increasing in a particular unit? Is there a spike in falls among post-operative patients? These insights allow leaders to intervene proactively, allocate resources strategically, and measure the impact of corrective actions.

Field Insight: Data is only powerful when it's actionable. Tracking systems must be designed for the people who use them—not just the people who analyze them.

Safety Event Review Teams (SERTs)

SERTs are multidisciplinary teams tasked with investigating safety events and developing actionable solutions. They bring together clinical experts, quality professionals, and frontline staff to conduct deep dives into incidents.

The goal is not to assign blame—it's to understand system failures and prevent recurrence.

A well-functioning SERT:

- **Reconstructs timelines** with precision and empathy.
- **Interviews involved parties** to gather context and insight.
- **Identifies contributing factors**—both technical and cultural.
- **Develops SMART action plans** that are tracked to completion.

SERTs should report findings to leadership and share lessons learned across the organization. Their work must be visible, valued, and validated.

Field Insight: SERTs are not just investigators—they are storytellers. They help the organization learn from its past to protect its future.

Root Cause Analysis (RCA) and Action Plans

RCA is a structured methodology for understanding why an adverse event occurred. It goes beyond surface-level explanations to uncover systemic issues.

Effective RCA involves:

- **Mapping the sequence of events** to understand what happened.
- **Identifying latent conditions and active failures** that contributed.
- **Engaging those closest to the work**—they hold the keys to insight.

- **Developing corrective actions** that address root causes, not just symptoms.

Action plans must be:

- **Embedded into workflows,** not just posted on bulletin boards.
- **Monitored for effectiveness,** with clear metrics and timelines.
- **Revisited regularly** to ensure sustainability and adaptation.

RCA is not just a tool—it's a mindset. It requires curiosity, humility, and a commitment to continuous improvement.

Field Insight: RCA is most powerful when it's participatory. When staff feel heard, they become part of the solution.

Executive and Board-Level Safety Reviews

Leadership engagement is critical. Executives and board members must be active participants in safety oversight. This means reviewing key metrics, asking hard questions, and holding teams accountable. It also means celebrating successes, recognizing staff contributions, and modeling a commitment to safety.

Board-level reviews should include:

- **Dashboards** that highlight trends and outliers.
- **Summaries of RCA findings** and follow-up actions.
- **Strategic discussions** that connect safety to financial outcomes, reputational risk, and long-term goals.

When safety is elevated to the boardroom, it becomes a core business priority—not just a clinical concern. It signals to the entire organization that safety is not negotiable—it's foundational.

Field Insight: Boards don't need to be experts in safety—they need to be champions of it.

Field Notes Where Transformation Becomes Real

Operationalizing the framework is where transformation becomes real. It's where systems align, behaviors shift, and outcomes improve. It requires discipline, transparency, and relentless focus—but the payoff is profound.

This step is not the end—it's the beginning. It's the moment when strategy becomes culture, and when every staff member becomes a steward of safety.

<u>Notes</u>

36

Chapter 6: Building Your Transformation Team

From Individuals to a Movement

No framework—no matter how elegant or evidence-based—can succeed without the right people behind it. Transformation is not a solo endeavor. It's a collective journey that demands vision, collaboration, and resilience. The most successful organizations don't just implement strategies—they cultivate teams that embody the mission and carry it forward with purpose.

In healthcare, where complexity is high and stakes are even higher, the strength of the team is everything. It's not just about assembling talent—it's about aligning values, building trust, and creating a shared sense of ownership. This chapter explores how to build, empower, and sustain a team capable of driving lasting change in patient safety and quality.

Defining Core Roles: The Pillars of Progress

Every transformation team is a mosaic of talent. It requires a blend of strategic thinkers, operational experts, and frontline champions—each bringing a unique lens to the challenge of improvement. These roles are not hierarchical—they are interdependent. Each one contributes to the system's ability to learn, adapt, and lead.

- **Chief Quality Officer (CQO)** The CQO is the architect of the vision. They set the strategic direction, ensure alignment with executive priorities, and serve as the public face of the initiative. Their role is both technical and symbolic—they must be fluent in safety science and capable of inspiring belief across the organization. They translate data into strategy and strategy into culture.

- **Frontline Champions:** These are the heartbeat of the transformation effort. Nurses, physicians, and allied health professionals who model safety behaviors, mentor peers, and provide real-time feedback. Their credibility comes from lived experience, and their influence is amplified by proximity to care. They are the eyes, ears, and conscience of the system.
- **Data Analysts and Improvement Specialists.** These individuals turn information into insight. They support root cause analysis (RCA), manage dashboards, and help teams interpret trends. Their work ensures that decisions are grounded in evidence, not intuition. They are the translators between numbers and narratives.
- **Executive Sponsors:** Transformation requires air cover. Executive sponsors provide resources, remove barriers, and ensure accountability at the highest levels. Their support signals that safety is not a side project—it's a strategic priority. They are the protectors of momentum and the champions of sustainability.

Field Insight: Each role must be clearly defined, supported with training, and empowered to lead. Ambiguity breeds inertia. Clarity fuels momentum.

Fostering Cross-Functional Collaboration: Breaking Down Silos

Quality and safety touch every corner of the organization—from the emergency department to the finance office. Success depends on breaking down silos and building bridges across disciplines. Collaboration is not a luxury—it's a necessity.

Key practices include:

- **Joint Rounds** When clinical and administrative leaders round together, they build shared understanding and mutual respect. These interactions foster empathy, align priorities, and surface insights that would otherwise remain hidden.

- **Shared Dashboards and Performance Reviews** Transparency drives accountability. When teams review performance together, they co-own the results—and the solutions. Shared data becomes a shared language.

- **Interdisciplinary Improvement Teams:** Complex challenges require diverse perspectives. Bringing together nurses, physicians, pharmacists, IT specialists, and others creates a richer problem-solving environment. These teams are not just functional—they are transformational.

Field Insight: Collaboration must be intentional. It doesn't happen by accident—it requires trust, shared goals, and a commitment to collective success.

Applying Change Management Principles: Leading Through Uncertainty

Transformation is change—and change is hard. It disrupts routines, challenges assumptions, and stirs resistance. That's why change management isn't a side project—it's the scaffolding that supports every initiative. Without it, even the best ideas will falter.

Proven strategies include:

- **Kotter's 8-Step Model** (Kotter, J.P. (1996) Leading Change. Harvard Business School Press, Boston. Kotter, J. P. (1995) Leading Change: Why Transformation Efforts Fail. Harvard Business Review, 73, 59-67). (Kotter, J. P. (1995). Leading Change: Why Transformation Efforts Fail ...") This classic framework emphasizes urgency, coalition-building, vision communication, and celebrating wins.

It's a roadmap for leading change with clarity and momentum.

- **ADKAR Framework** (Hiatt, J. (2006). "ADKAR: A Model for Change in Business, Government and Our Community." ("ADKAR by Jeffrey M. Hiatt | Summary, Quotes, FAQ, Audio") Prosci Research). ADKAR focuses on the individual journey through change: Awareness, Desire, Knowledge, Ability, and Reinforcement. ("The 5 Steps to Successful Change: Understanding the ADKAR Model") It reminds us that transformation happens one person at a time—and that each person's journey matters.

- **Psychological Safety** Teams must feel safe to speak up, experiment, and learn from failure. Without psychological safety, innovation stalls and fear takes root. Leaders must model vulnerability, reward candor, and protect dissent.

Field Insight: Change management is not a checklist—it's a mindset. It requires empathy, persistence, and the ability to navigate ambiguity with grace.

Field Notes: The Human Side of Transformation

The most successful teams are those that combine technical expertise with emotional intelligence. They listen deeply, learn continuously, and lead with humility. They celebrate progress, mourn setbacks, and stay grounded in the mission.

They understand that transformation is not about systems or metrics—it's about people. It's about the nurse who notices a subtle change in a patient's condition, the technician who speaks up during a procedure, the administrator who refuses to accept "good enough." It's about building a culture where excellence is expected and where every voice matters.

Building such a team is not easy—but it is essential. Because when people come together with purpose, anything is possible.

Notes

42

Chapter 7: Leadership and Culture—The Engine of Safety

Why People, Not Protocols, Drive Patient Safety

Patient safety is often misunderstood as a technical challenge—something that can be solved with checklists, dashboards, and quarterly reports. But in reality, safety is a human endeavor. It lives in the choices people make, the conversations they have, and the values they uphold. It is a living, breathing culture—and leadership is its heartbeat.

To build a truly safe healthcare system, we must look beyond metrics and into the soul of the organization. This chapter explores how leadership and culture form the invisible engine that powers sustainable safety.

The Anatomy of Safety Leadership: Presence Over Position

True safety leadership is not about titles or hierarchy—it's about presence. It's about showing up, listening deeply, and modeling the behaviors that create trust. The most effective safety leaders are not always found in the boardroom. They're on the floor, in the break room, and at the bedside.

They are:

- The department head who rounds with humility, asking questions instead of giving orders.
- The nurse manager who listens without judgment and follows up with action.
- The CEO who knows the name of the environmental services worker and asks how their day is going.

Safety leaders:

- Model transparency, even when the truth is uncomfortable.
- Invite dissent, knowing that silence is more dangerous than disagreement.
- Celebrate reporting, not just resolution.
- Ask "what went wrong?", but also "what went right—and why?"

Field Insight: Culture is not built in boardrooms—it's built in break rooms, hallways, and huddles. Leadership is not a title—it's a behavior.

Psychological Safety: The Invisible Infrastructure

If people don't feel safe to speak up, nothing else matters. Psychological safety is the invisible infrastructure of high-performing teams. It's what allows a junior resident to question a senior surgeon, or a housekeeper to report a spill before someone slips.

Creating psychological safety requires:

- Consistent responses to error—never punitive, always curious.
- Rituals of reflection—debriefs, huddles, and storytelling that normalize vulnerability.
- Leaders who admit their own mistakes modeling humility and openness.

Without psychological safety, safety initiatives become theater—performative gestures that fail to penetrate the culture. With it, they become movement—organic, resilient, and deeply rooted.

Field Insight: Psychological safety is not a luxury—it's a prerequisite. It's the soil in which every safety initiative must be planted.

Culture as a Strategic Asset

Culture is often dismissed as "soft"—something intangible, emotional, and secondary to strategy. But in reality, it's the hardest thing to build and the most powerful lever for change.

Organizations with strong safety cultures:

- Have higher reporting rates—a sign of trust, not failure.
- Experience fewer adverse events—because problems are surfaced early.
- Retain staff longer and burn out less—because people feel valued and heard.

Culture is not a side effect—it's a strategy. It must be cultivated with intention, reinforced through rituals, and protected through leadership.

Field Insight: Culture is not what you say—it's what you tolerate. It's not a mood—it's a system.

The Role of Middle Management: Translators of Vision

Middle managers are the unsung heroes of transformation. They carry the message from the C-suite to the bedside. They translate strategy into action and values into behaviors. If they're not engaged, the strategy dies in the middle.

Empowering middle managers means:

- Giving them data they can act on, not just dashboards they can't influence.
- Training them in coaching, not just compliance.
- Recognizing their role as culture carriers, not just task managers.

They are the bridge—and they must be fortified.

Field Insight: Middle managers are the pulse of the organization. If they're thriving, the culture is thriving.

Leading Through Crisis: Character Revealed

The COVID-19 pandemic tested every assumption about leadership. It revealed who was prepared, who was adaptable, and who was willing to lead with empathy. In times of crisis, safety leaders:

- Communicate frequently, even when the message is incomplete.
- Prioritize staff well-being as fiercely as patient outcomes.
- Make decisions with moral clarity, not just operational efficiency.

Crisis doesn't build character—it reveals it. And the leaders who emerged strongest were those who led with compassion, transparency, and courage.

Field Insight: In crisis, people don't need perfection—they need presence.

Field Notes: The Engine of Safety

Leadership and culture are not accessories to safety—they are its engine. When that engine runs on trust, transparency, and compassion, it can power extraordinary change. But it must be fueled daily—through conversations, decisions, and behaviors that reflect the values we claim to hold.

Safety is not a checklist. It's a commitment. And it begins with how we lead.

Notes

Chapter 8: Case Studies and Success Stories

Turning Theory into Practice, and Practice into Progress

Theory provides the scaffolding for change—but stories breathe life into it. Case studies are more than anecdotes; they are proof of concept. They illuminate the messy realities of transformation, the setbacks and breakthroughs, and the human spirit that drives improvement. They show us that change is not just possible—it's already happening, in places big and small, well-resourced and under-resourced, urban and rural.

This chapter presents three distinct journeys—each offering valuable lessons about leadership, culture, and the power of intentional action.

<u>Case Study 1</u>: A Rural Hospital's Journey to Safety

Trust Over Technology

In a quiet Appalachian town, a 75-bed community hospital was grappling with rising adverse events, declining staff morale, and a pervasive sense of helplessness. With no formal quality department and limited financial resources, the situation seemed bleak. But the leadership team made a bold, counterintuitive decision: instead of investing in expensive tools, they invested in people.

They began with daily safety huddles—brief, structured conversations where staff could surface concerns, share observations, and coordinate responses. Every employee, from physicians to dietary aides, was trained in Just Culture principles, reinforcing the idea that errors are opportunities for learning, not punishment.

The results were staggering:

- Reporting rates increased by 100% within six months—a sign that staff felt safe to speak up.
- Adverse events dropped by 40% by year's end.
- Patient satisfaction scores reached their highest levels in a decade.

This transformation wasn't driven by dashboards or algorithms—it was driven by trust. When staff felt heard and supported, they became active participants in safety. The hospital didn't just improve outcomes—it rebuilt its culture from the inside out.

Lesson: Safety doesn't require scale—it requires sincerity. Even the smallest institutions can lead with courage and create lasting change.

<u>**Case Study 2**</u>: A Multi-Hospital System Harnesses Predictive Analytics

Data With Purpose

A regional health system spanning five hospitals and dozens of outpatient clinics was facing a persistent challenge: preventable readmissions. Despite adherence to clinical protocols and discharge planning, patients kept returning—costing millions and eroding trust.

Rather than doubling down on existing workflows, the system invested in predictive analytics, using machine learning to flag patients at high risk for readmission before they left the hospital. But the real innovation wasn't the algorithm—it was the action it enabled.

- Care coordinators were assigned to flagged patients, ensuring continuity of care.
- Follow-up calls were standardized to check on medication adherence, symptoms, and social needs.

- Home health referrals were streamlined, reducing gaps in post-discharge support.

Within 12 months:

- Readmissions dropped by 18%.
- The system saved over $3 million in avoidable costs.
- Staff reported greater confidence in discharge planning and patient engagement.

This case illustrates that data alone doesn't drive change—data in the hands of empowered teams does. The analytics didn't replace human judgment; they enhanced it.

Lesson: Technology is a tool, not a solution. Its value lies in how it enables people to act with precision and compassion.

<u>Case Study 3</u>: Lessons from a Failed Implementation

Culture Before Tools

At a prestigious academic medical center, a new safety initiative was launched with great anticipation. The framework was sound, the tools were sophisticated, and the branding was polished. But within months, the effort stalled.

- Reporting rates remained low.
- Frontline staff felt excluded.
- Leadership engagement was sporadic.

A candid postmortem revealed the root cause: the initiative had been designed in isolation, without meaningful input from those closest to the work. It was a top-down solution to a bottom-up problem.

In response, the center rebooted the program—this time co-designing it with nurses, residents, and support staff. Psychological safety became a cornerstone. Feedback loops were built into every phase. Leaders showed up—not just for meetings, but for conversations.

The second launch succeeded—not because the tools changed, but because the culture did. Staff felt ownership. Leaders felt accountability. The initiative became a shared mission, not a mandate.

Lesson: Even the best tools fail in the wrong culture. Inclusion isn't a courtesy—it's a requirement for success.

Field Notes: The Arc of Transformation

Success is rarely linear. It requires humility, iteration, and a willingness to listen. These stories remind us that transformation is not reserved for the well-resourced—it belongs to the bold. It's not about perfection—it's about persistence.

Whether in a rural hospital, a sprawling health system, or a world-renowned academic center, the principles remain the same: trust your people, act on your data, and build your culture with intention.

Notes

52

Chapter 9: Innovation and Continuous Improvement

Fueling Transformation Through Curiosity, Courage, and Change

Innovation is the oxygen of transformation. In healthcare, where complexity is high and stakes are even higher, standing still is not an option. The systems that once sustained us are now being reimagined. The question is no longer *if* we should innovate—but *how*, *where*, and *with whom*.

Innovation is not a luxury reserved for well-funded institutions or cutting-edge labs. It is a necessity for every organization committed to delivering safer, smarter, and more equitable care. It is the bridge between what we know and what we could become. And it must be continuous—not episodic, not reactive, but embedded into the DNA of how we work, learn, and lead.

This chapter explores how organizations can harness emerging technologies, elevate patient voices, and scale best practices to create a culture where improvement is not a project—it's a way of being.

Emerging Technologies: Tools That Think, See, and Predict

Technology is no longer a supporting actor—it's a protagonist in the story of modern healthcare. But its power lies not in novelty, but in its ability to solve real problems, enhance human judgment, and extend care beyond traditional boundaries.

- **Artificial Intelligence (AI)** has moved from the margins to the mainstream. Predictive analytics now flag sepsis risk hours before symptoms appear. Natural language processing extracts insights from unstructured clinical notes, surfacing trends that would otherwise remain hidden. These tools don't replace clinicians—they augment them, offering sharper lenses and faster feedback. When deployed thoughtfully, AI becomes a partner in care, not a replacement.

- **Remote Monitoring Tools** Wearables, sensors, and mobile apps are redefining the care continuum. Patients can track their vitals, report symptoms, and receive alerts—all from home. This reduces unnecessary visits, enables early interventions, and empowers patients to take an active role in their health. It also shifts the locus of care from the hospital to the home, expanding reach and reducing burden.

- **Digital Twins and Virtual Simulations** Digital twins—virtual models of patient pathways—allow teams to test interventions before deploying them. Want to redesign a discharge process? Simulate it first. These tools offer a safe space to innovate, fail, and refine—without risking patient harm. They also foster interdisciplinary collaboration, allowing clinicians, administrators, and technologists to co-design solutions in real time.

Field Insight: Technology alone is not enough. It must be deployed ethically, equitably, and with a relentless focus on usability. If it doesn't work for the frontline, it doesn't work at all.

Patient Engagement: From Passive Recipient to Active Partner

Patients are not passive—they are experts in their own lives. Engaging them in safety and quality initiatives isn't just respectful—it's strategic. When patients are involved, outcomes improve, trust deepens, and care becomes more personalized.

- **Co-Designing Care Plans** Instead of prescribing solutions, invite patients to shape them. What matters to them? What barriers do they face? Co-designed plans lead to better adherence and more meaningful outcomes. They also foster dignity, autonomy, and shared accountability.

- **Patient Safety Committees** Patients can and should serve on safety committees, offering insights that clinicians may overlook. Their lived experience adds depth to discussions and keeps the focus on what truly matters. It also challenges assumptions and surfaces blind spots.

- **Feedback on RCA Processes** When patients contribute to root cause analyses, they help uncover blind spots and humanize the data. Their stories turn statistics into catalysts for change. They remind us that behind every metric is a person—and behind every person is a story worth listening to.

Field Insight: This shift—from "doing to" to "doing with"—is not cosmetic. It's transformational. It redefines the power dynamic and builds a system that listens, learns, and evolves.

Scaling Best Practices: From Pilot to Systemwide Impact

Innovation is only as powerful as its reach. A successful pilot in one unit is a start—but the real challenge is scaling that success across the organization. This requires discipline, infrastructure, and adaptability.

Key enablers include:

- **Standardized Protocols:** Clear, replicable processes ensure consistency and reduce variation. But standardization must leave room for local nuance. Flexibility within a framework is key.

- **Training Programs:** Teams need the skills to implement new practices. Training should be hands-on, interdisciplinary, and ongoing. It should build confidence, not just competence.

- **Fidelity Monitoring:** Are teams following the protocol as intended? Fidelity checks ensure that innovation doesn't drift or dilute over time. They also provide feedback loops for refinement.
- **Leadership Support** Scaling requires champions at every level. Leaders must allocate resources, remove barriers, and celebrate progress. They must model commitment and reward courage.

Field Insight: Scaling is not just about replication—it's about adaptation. Each context is unique, and best practices must be tailored accordingly. Flexibility is as important as fidelity.

Field Notes Innovation as a Way of Being

Innovation is not a department—it's a mindset. It thrives in environments that reward curiosity, tolerate failure, and celebrate learning. It's not reserved for tech startups or academic centers—it belongs in every clinic, every ward, every conversation.

To innovate is to ask: *What if?*

To improve is to ask: *What next?*

To transform is to ask: *Who else can we bring along?*

Innovation is not about chasing the new—it's about solving the now. It's about seeing problems as invitations, constraints as creative prompts, and setbacks as stepping stones. It's about building a culture where improvement is not episodic—but continuous.

And it starts with people. With the nurse who questions a protocol, the physician who pilots a new workflow, and the patient who shares a story that changes everything.

Innovation is not a destination—it's a discipline. And it's within reach.

Notes

Chapter 10: Equity, Ethics, and the Future of Safety

Reimagining Safety as a Moral Imperative

As healthcare systems evolve and technologies advance, the frontier of patient safety continues to expand. But progress without conscience is hollow. Safety is not merely a clinical benchmark—it is a moral obligation. It demands that we protect *every* patient, not just the average one. It requires that we confront uncomfortable truths, dismantle systemic barriers, and build a future where safety is not a privilege—but a right.

This chapter explores how equity and ethics must be embedded into the very DNA of safety, and how leadership must rise to meet the moment with clarity, courage, and compassion. Because the future of safety is not just about doing things right—it's about doing the right things.

Addressing Disparities: Seeing What's Been Overlooked

Disparities in healthcare outcomes are not anomalies—they are signals. They reveal where systems fall short, where bias creeps in, and where access is uneven. They are not just statistical outliers—they are moral failures. To address them, we must first *see* them.

- **Disaggregating Data**: Aggregate metrics can mask inequities. By breaking down outcomes by race, ethnicity, income, geography, language, and other social determinants, we uncover patterns that demand attention. For example, are readmission rates higher among non-English speakers? Are pain scores underreported in certain racial groups? These insights are the first step toward justice.

- **Designing Targeted Interventions**: Equity is not achieved through blanket solutions. It requires tailored strategies—community health workers who speak the language, transportation vouchers for rural patients, and culturally competent care models that honor lived experience. It means meeting people where they are, not where we wish they were.

- **Investing in Representation and Partnership**: Diverse teams bring diverse perspectives. Hiring staff who reflect the communities they serve fosters trust and improves care. Partnering with local organizations ensures that interventions are grounded in reality, not assumptions. Equity is not just about access—it's about belonging.

Field Insight: Equity begins with humility—the willingness to ask hard questions and the courage to act on the answers. It's not a metric—it's a mindset.

Ethical Use of Data: Power with Responsibility

Data is the lifeblood of modern safety science. It drives decisions, shapes interventions, and predicts risk. But with great data comes great responsibility. As predictive models and AI tools become more prevalent, we must ensure that their use is ethical, transparent, and fair.

- **Transparency and Validation**: Predictive algorithms must be explainable. Clinicians and patients alike should understand how decisions are made. Models must be rigorously validated across diverse populations to avoid perpetuating bias. If we don't know how a model works, we shouldn't use it.

- **Informed and Ongoing Consent** Patients must know how their data is being used—not just at the point of collection, but throughout its lifecycle. Consent should be revisited, not assumed. Autonomy is not a checkbox—it's a principle.

- **Privacy and Autonomy**: Data must be protected with the highest standards of security. Patients must retain control over their information, and their autonomy must be respected in every decision. Safety without privacy is not safety—it's surveillance.

- **Algorithmic Auditing** Bias doesn't always announce itself. Regular audits of algorithms are essential to ensure fairness, especially as models evolve and are applied in new contexts. Equity must be engineered into the system—not retrofitted after harm occurs.

Field Insight: Ethics is not a checkbox—it's a compass. It guides not just what we do, but *how* and *why* we do it. It's the difference between compliance and conscience.

Leadership in a Post-Pandemic World: Humanity at the Helm

The COVID-19 pandemic was a crucible. It exposed vulnerabilities, accelerated innovation, and redefined resilience. It also revealed the true nature of leadership—not as a position, but as a presence. In this new era, safety leaders must be more than strategic—they must be deeply human.

In this new landscape, leaders must:

- **Communicate with Clarity and Frequency**: Even when the message is incomplete, transparency builds trust. Silence breeds fear—communication fosters connection. Leaders must speak often, listen more, and admit what they don't know.

- **Prioritize Staff Well-Being:** Burnout is a safety issue. Leaders must invest in mental health resources, flexible scheduling, and recognition programs that honor the emotional labor of caregiving. A resilient workforce is not a luxury—it's a prerequisite.

- **Prepare for Future Disruptions:** Resilience is not reactive—it's proactive. Scenario planning, cross-training, and robust contingency protocols are no longer optional. The next crisis is not a question of *if*—but *when*.

- **Lead With Empathy and Moral Clarity:** Decisions must be guided not just by efficiency, but by ethics. Leaders must ask: *What is the right thing to do—even if it's the hardest?* They must model courage, protect dissent, and elevate the voices of those closest to the work.

Field Insight: The future of safety depends on leaders who are not just strategic—but deeply human. Leadership is not about control—it's about connection.

Field Notes Building a Future Worth Trusting

Equity and ethics are not add-ons—they are the foundation. They are the lens through which every safety initiative must be viewed. They are not constraints—they are catalysts. The future of safety is:

- **Inclusive**—designed with and for diverse communities.
- **Transparent**—grounded in honesty and accountability.
- **Adaptive**—ready to evolve as new challenges emerge.

This future is not built by algorithms or dashboards alone. It is built by people—by those who choose to lead with empathy, act with integrity, and innovate with purpose. It is built by teams who ask better questions, listen more deeply, and refuse to accept "good enough."

Because safety is not just about doing things right—it's about doing the right things.

Closing Remarks: The Frontier Is You

A Call to Courage, Curiosity, and Collective Action

Transformation is not a destination—it's a journey. And it doesn't begin with a policy memo, a strategic plan, or a new dashboard. It begins with a person. It begins with *you.*

Throughout this book, we've explored frameworks, tools, and stories that illuminate the path to safer, more equitable, and more effective care. We've examined systems, dissected failures, and celebrated breakthroughs. But the real power—the force that drives change—is not found in diagrams or directives. It's found in people. In their choices, their questions, and their courage.

Whether you're a nurse on the night shift who notices a subtle change in a patient's condition, a CEO in the boardroom deciding where to invest limited resources, or a care manager fighting for dignity and transparency, you are part of the *Frontier*. You are shaping the future of healthcare every time you choose to speak up, to listen, to learn, and to lead.

The Power of Questions

Transformation begins with inquiry. With the courage to ask:

- *Why did this happen?*
- *What could we do differently?*
- *Who wasn't at the table—and why?*

Better questions lead to better systems. They challenge assumptions, uncover blind spots, and open doors to innovation. They shift the conversation from blame to learning, from silence to action.

The Courage to Build

You have the ability to build safer systems—not just through technology, but through trust. Every checklist, every huddle, every moment of reflection is a brick in the foundation of a culture that protects and uplifts. You don't need permission to care deeply. You just need conviction.

Safety is not a department—it's a daily practice. It's the quiet decision to double-check, to speak up, to stay curious. It's the belief that better is always possible—and that you have a role in making it so.

The Choice to Lead with Humanity

Empathy is not a soft skill—it's a strategic advantage. ("The Human Elements in Auditing: Building Trust and Professional ...") Integrity is not a luxury—it's a necessity. Innovation is not reserved for the few—it belongs to the curious, the persistent, and the brave. Leadership is not defined by title—it's defined by behavior.

In every moment of care, there is a choice: to rush or to listen, to dismiss or to engage, to protect the status quo or to challenge it. The leaders who shape the future will be those who choose humanity—again and again.

The *Frontier* Is Not Fixed

The frontier of quality and safety is not a line on a map—it's a living edge that expands every time someone chooses to act with purpose. It grows when a resident asks a hard question, when a technician reports a near miss, when a patient shares their story. It grows when we choose progress over perfection, and people over process.

This *Frontier* is not reserved for experts or executives. It belongs to everyone who believes that healthcare can—and must— do better.

A Shared Mission

So go forward. Be bold in your vision. Be curious in your pursuit. Be relentless in your commitment. The work ahead is not easy—but it is essential. And you are not alone.

Together, we can make healthcare safer, smarter, and more human. Not someday. Not somewhere else. But here. Now.

The *Frontier* is you.

A Personal Thank You

Thank you for reading this book. Thank you for caring enough to ask hard questions, to challenge assumptions, and to imagine a better way. Whether you're just beginning your journey or have been leading change for years, I hope this framework has offered you clarity, courage, and companionship.

This work is not mine alone—it belongs to all of us. ("Feeling Emotional. | Aradhana Dubey | 14 comments") And I'm honored to walk this path with you.

—Dr. A.H. Nguyen

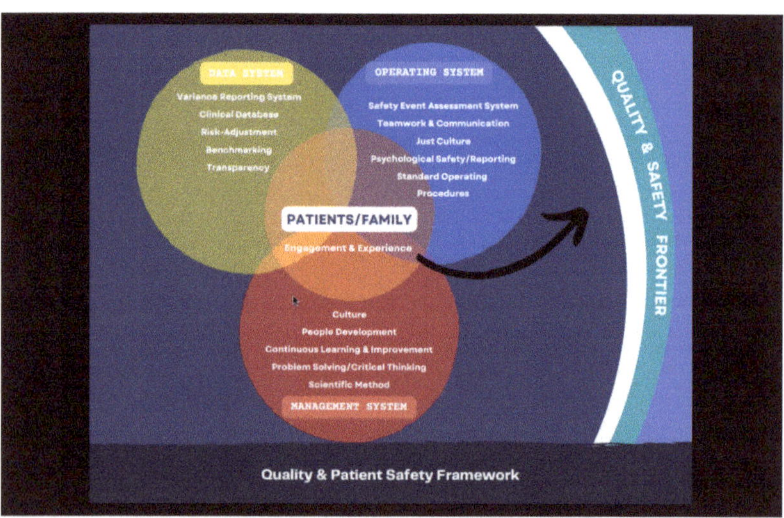